THE
TERRIBLE TALES
OF
HAPPY DAYS
SCHOOL

THE
TERRIBLE TALES
OF
HAPPY DAYS
SCHOOL

by
Lois Duncan

Illustrated by
Friso Henstra

LITTLE, BROWN AND COMPANY
BOSTON   TORONTO

I write these tales for my son, Don.
No wonder I am tired and wan!
Each of his friends may find a nook
Within the pages of this book.

TEXT COPYRIGHT © 1983 BY LOIS DUNCAN

ILLUSTRATIONS COPYRIGHT © 1983 BY FRISO HENSTRA

ALL RIGHTS RESERVED. NO PART OF THIS BOOK MAY BE REPRODUCED
IN ANY FORM OR BY ANY ELECTRONIC OR MECHANICAL MEANS INCLUDING
INFORMATION STORAGE AND RETRIEVAL SYSTEMS WITHOUT PERMISSION
IN WRITING FROM THE PUBLISHER, EXCEPT BY A REVIEWER
WHO MAY QUOTE BRIEF PASSAGES IN A REVIEW.

FIRST EDITION

Library of Congress Cataloging in Publication Data

Duncan, Lois, 1934–
    The terrible tales of Happy Days School.

    Summary: The students at Happy Days Progressive
School, allowed to do whatever they please, are
happy to do so until the school must close for
lack of students.
    [1. Stories in rhyme.   2. School stories.
3. Behavior — Fiction]   I. Title.
PZ8.3.D9158Te   1983   [Fic]   82-14945
ISBN 0-316-19541-3

BP

Published simultaneously in Canada
by Little, Brown and Company (Canada) Limited

PRINTED IN THE UNITED STATES OF AMERICA

ROSTER OF FORMER STUDENTS
AT
HAPPY DAYS PROGRESSIVE SCHOOL

JANE

MELISSA

SAM

ART

BELINDA

DAN

JEROME

NANCY

HUGH

MARY LOU

JAMES

PROLOGUE

At Happy Days Progressive School
There was one single, standing rule —
That all the children going there
Be given gentle, loving care
And never ever forced to do
A thing unless they wanted to.
How happy all those students were!
There wasn't one who did prefer
The public school a block away
Where children had to *work* all day.
The school stayed open just one year.
Why it was closed was not made clear,
But when that year came to its ending
The children simply weren't attending.
How strange! For all had words of praise
For that fine school called Happy Days.

JANE

"I will not eat this stuff!" cried Jane.
"This cafeteria food's a pain!
The pork's so gross I will not stick
My fork in it! I might be sick!
The roll is hard! The beans are cold!
The milk tastes sour! The salad's old!"
She grabbed her plate, then spun around
And with an awful, retching sound
She threw its contents on the floor.
The principal came through the door,
Stepped on the food and took a slide.
His arms flung out, his legs spread wide,
He plowed full speed into a wall,
And then he did not move at all.
The cafeteria lady cried,
"My dear, if you're not satisfied,
Give back your milk so others may
Have seconds if they wish to pay."
Jane snatched her milk. With evil grin
She caved the cardboard carton in.
She stamped upon each slimy bean
Until the floor was slick and green.
She kicked her roll, and, with a shout,
She watched it knock a window out,
And then she jumped into the mess
(Why she would do that, who can guess),
And hit a greasy gravy trail.
Her laughter turned into a wail.
She fell and landed on her fork.
She should have left it in the pork.

9

MELISSA

Melissa flew into a rage.
She shrieked, "I will not clean that cage!"
Her mother said, "Now, dear, remember
The talk we had back last September?
If we bought pets, you promised us
You'd care for them without a fuss."
Melissa snarled a nasty word
I can't believe her parents heard.
She turned her back, and off she went.
Her mother's pleas made not a dent.
As weeks went by the cage grew rank.
It smelled just like a septic tank.
The litter turned from brown to green.
The hamsters wished that it were clean
So they could run and play in it,
But all the poor things did was sit
High in their wheel and gasp for air.
It was an awful thing to bear!
Melissa in her thoughtless way
Passed by the cage and stopped one day
To glance inside. I don't know why.
Just then her brother, Sam, walked by
And pinched her hard. She gave a yell!
Her feet flew up, and in she fell!
She landed in the molding litter
And all the hamsters ran and bit her.
The gerbils rushed to bite her too,
And how those little things could chew!
The child was such an awful mess
Her mother had to burn her dress.

SAM

And what of Sam, who with intent
Produced his sister's accident?
Sam loved to pinch. He did it hard,
So all his friends were bruised and scarred.
His mother had a painful place
Upon the left side of her face
Where Sam one day in fit of pique
Had sunk his nails into her cheek.
His father, with a tougher skin,
When Sam attacked tried hard to grin
And act as though his playful son
Was only out to have some fun.
At recess time Sam's favorite thing
Was pinching people on the swing.
As it swung gently back and forth
From north to south — from south to north —
Sam stood behind with clawed hand high
To pinch his friends as they swung by.
The girls would squeal and sometimes leap
And tumble off and start to weep.
Sam laughed aloud. He liked that fine.
"And now," he'd cry, "the swing is mine!"
One day he pinched a boy named Art
Upon a man's most tender part.
Art did not yell. He did not fall.
He kicked out hard, and that was all
As he swung north. As he swung south
His foot struck Sammy in the mouth.
Sam's teeth went spattering far and wide
Except for three that stayed inside.

ART

Art's hobby was collecting things,
Like other people's diamond rings,
And ten-speed bikes that were not locked
(Some bikes he kept, and some he hocked),
The hubcaps from his neighbors' cars,
And chewing gum and candy bars
When they were set out on display
And Safeway owners looked away.
Art's room at home was filled with toys
That once belonged to other boys.
His parents were not very smart.
They didn't think to question Art.
They simply said, "How nice to know
Our Artie's classmates love him so.
He doesn't even know their names,
Yet they all give him toys and games."
So Art's immense collection grew.
It filled one room. Then it filled two.
The closets bulged. The whole floor sagged
Beneath the loot that Art had bagged,
But still he brought home more and more
From every dime and discount store.
His teachers never once suspected
How many things Art had collected
From lockers, desks and students' pockets
Until the day he stole the sockets
From floor lamps in a hotel lobby.
That was the end of Artie's hobby.
As sparks flew high and fuses blew,
It was the end of Artie too.

BELINDA

Belinda's hobby was to chew.
A simple gumball would not do;
She liked to nibble solid things
Like books and balls and yo-yo strings
And anything made out of wood.
She thought that pencils tasted good,
Preferring those with colored leads
And rubber tips that fell in shreds.
Above all else, she loved her nails,
As pale and thick as shells on snails.
They had not always been that way.
(You chew enough, and nails turn gray.)
Whenever she got bored in class,
Belinda's hobby helped time pass.
Her teachers smiled and said, "How great
To see a student concentrate!"
One day, while studying for a test,
Which was the time nails tasted best,
Belinda got so lost in chewing
She quite forgot what she was doing
And gnawed and gnashed and smacked her lips
Until she ate her fingertips.
They just went "Crunch" and disappeared.
Belinda thought, "Now this is weird!
I wonder why that knucklebone
Is sticking up there all alone?"
Her parents were not pleased at all
When they received her frantic call.
To re-grow fingertips is rare,
So now Belinda chews her hair.

DAN

At Happy Days the smartest child
Was one who drove his parents wild.
His name was Dan. He knew a lot.
The information that he got
Was from the things he overheard.
His parents couldn't say a word
In privacy, for Dan would hide
To hear what things they might confide.
He hid behind a Morris chair
And learned his mother dyed her hair.
He hid beneath the kitchen sink
And learned his father liked to drink.
He even found a secret place
To watch them playing kissy-face.
He learned so much he filled a book
With all the detailed notes he took
And even used a tape recorder
To keep his facts in perfect order.
His teachers thought that Dan was super
Despite the fact he was a snooper.
They said, "He does contribute well,
Especially at show-and-tell."
One day Dan's mother's Auntie Bea
Came over for a cup of tea.
Dan thought, "Now I can have some sport!"
He hid beneath the davenport
So he could eavesdrop on their chat.
His Auntie's rear was huge and fat.
The sofa caved beneath its weight
And Dan was squashed flat as a plate.

JEROME

Jerome disliked to wash his face
Or, really, any other place.
There were deposits in his ears
That had been rotting there for years.
His neck and chest were quickly crusting,
His belly button was disgusting,
And there was nothing very sweet
About the odor of his feet.
His parents begged him, "Please, Jerome,
Just use a toothbrush and a comb!"
"That's not my bag," Jerome replied.
"At Happy Days it's what's inside
That matters, not the outer shell.
Who cares how people look and smell?"
One morning in the early spring
Jerome observed a funny thing.
Between his toes were tiny shoots
Which overnight had put down roots,
And both the pits beneath his arms
Were sprouting up like little farms.
Jerome grew slightly nervous now.
He said, "I'd rather wash than plow,"
And climbed into the nearest shower.
The dirt washed off in half an hour,
But since the grime adhered like glue
The skin beneath it came off too.
It's hard to keep your insides in
When you are left without your skin,
So with an anguished shriek of pain
All of Jerome went down the drain.

21

NANCY

When Nancy walked to school each day
She passed the home of Mr. Gray,
And in his fenced front yard she'd see
A puppy dog tied to a tree.
Thought Nancy, "It would be a lark
If I could make that puppy bark."
She saw a stone and picked it up,
Took aim, and threw it at the pup.
The puppy yipped and tried to run,
And Nancy cried, "Hey, this is fun!"
From that time on each time she'd pass
And see the puppy on the grass
She'd hit it with a stone or stick
To make it do its barking trick.
The tiny dog would howl and yelp,
Which was its way to call for help,
But Mr. Gray was shut inside
And did not hear it when it cried.
The weeks went by. The months did, too.
The frightened little puppy grew
Into a dog quite large and strong.
One day when Nancy came along,
Her pockets full of stones to hurl,
She learned her lesson, wretched girl.
The dog had gnawed its rope in two
(A thing she thought it could not do),
And by the time she had the sense
To turn and run, it leaped the fence
And chewed her till she came apart,
And ate her liver and her heart.

23

HUGH

Hugh liked to lie. He did it well.
What splendid stories he could tell!
He told his little sister Anne
About a huge gorilla man
Who entered houses with a leap.
The poor child screamed herself to sleep.
He told his baby brother Don
There was a monster in the john
Who snatched small boys and pulled them down
Beneath the water so they'd drown.
He filled the kid so full of fears
He was not potty trained for years.
At school his storytelling powers
Kept classmates entertained for hours.
His teacher said, "Imagination
Like this predicts some great vocation."
One evening rather close to dark
Hugh told a stranger in the park
His father was a millionaire.
The man grabbed Hughie by the hair
And kidnapped him. He made Hugh write
To tell his parents of his plight.
"You'll have to pay," the letter said,
"A ransom or I will be dead!"
His parents chuckled, "Oh, that Hugh!
We know his tales are never true."
They threw the letter in the trash
And never sent a bit of cash.
They've not seen Hughie to this day.
They think perhaps he ran away.

MARY LOU

When Mary Lou began to eat
Her family had a special treat.
They got to watch her slurp and slop
And dribble on the tabletop.
She never touched the silverware
Her mother placed so nicely there.
Instead she'd scoop with greedy paws
Great dripping loads of applesauce
And mashed potatoes, wet and sticky,
And Cream of Wheat (she wasn't picky),
Toss back her head, and cram them down.
Such manners made her parents frown.
"I hate to nag you, Mary Lou,"
Her father said, "but if you chew
It might be easier to swallow."
Such reasoning was hard to follow.
Said Mary Lou, "I swallow fine
Whenever I sit down to dine."
She grabbed two greasy chicken legs
And covered them with scrambled eggs
And loaded on some onion fries
(Her parents gagged and closed their eyes),
And then as quickly as a wink
She dipped them in her orange drink,
Threw wide her mouth, and down they went.
The chicken legs weren't even bent!
One tragic evening while she ate
Her jawbone snapped beneath the weight
Of seven quarts of Irish stew.
So, no dessert for Mary Lou.

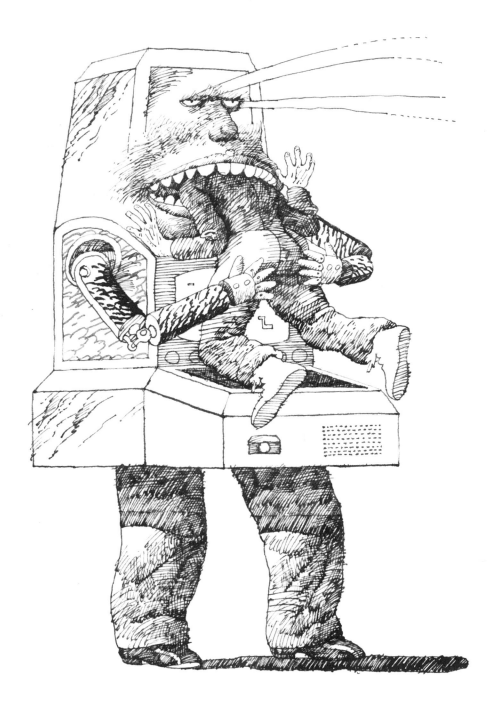

JAMES

At Happy Days, a boy named James
Was really into video games.
When lunchtime came, James did not eat.
Instead, he raced across the street
Into the Jolly Times Arcade
And shut the door, and there he stayed.
He started out with little frogs
That hopped across a stream on logs.
He didn't find that too inspiring,
And so he moved to missile firing,
And then went searching for a place
Where he could slaughter men from space.
James found a flight of stairs that wound
Down to some rooms beneath the ground.
Into these depths he made his way
To find new games that he could play.
With every turn he made, he'd find
A larger game. It blew his mind!
Each was more thrilling than the one
That came before. James cried, "What fun!
I'll play them all! I'll never leave!"
He felt a hand tug at his sleeve
And turned to find a monster standing
Beside him on the stairway landing.
Its jaws gaped wide! Its eyes shot flames!
Alas, there was no hope for James.
The game machines made so much noise
That no one heard his screaming voice,
And no one heard the painful crunch
As Pac-Man had an early lunch.

EPILOGUE

The year was done. School was dismissed.
The principal's attendance list
Was oddly blank. He scratched his head.
"This is so very strange," he said.
"Our students seemed to have such fun,
And yet we've lost them one by one."
The registration forms were piled
Upon his desk, but not a child
Had signed up for the coming year.
"Well, Happy Days must close, I fear,"
He told the teachers with a sigh.
"It is enough to make one cry.
I simply cannot understand
The failure of a school so grand."
And so he shut and locked the door.

And no one goes there anymore.